Level 2 is ideal for chil~~dren who have~~ received
some reading instructio~~n~~ ~~and short,~~
simple sentences with h

Special features:

story wor~~ds~~

Short,
simple
sentences

Once there was
a happy princess.

She loved to play by the
river with her golden ball.

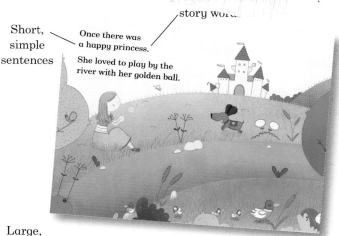

6   7

Large,
clear type

One day, the golden ball
fell into the river.

Just then, up jumped a frog.

"If I get your ball back, will
you make me a promise?"
he said.

Careful match
between
story and
pictures

8   9

Educational Consultant: Geraldine Taylor
Book Banding Consultant: Kate Ruttle

A catalogue record for this book is available from the British Library

Published by Ladybird Books Ltd
80 Strand, London, WC2R 0RL
A Penguin Company

009
© LADYBIRD BOOKS LTD MMXIV
Ladybird, Read It Yourself and the Ladybird Logo are registered or
unregistered trademarks of Ladybird Books Limited.

ISBN: 978-0-72328-060-6

Printed in China

The Princess and the Frog

Illustrated by Marta Cabrol

Once there was
a happy princess.

She loved to play by the
river with her golden ball.

6

7

One day, the golden ball
fell into the river.

Just then, up jumped a frog.

"If I get your ball back, will
you make me a promise?"
he said.

"I will," the princess promised.

"You must let me sit with you, eat with you and sleep on your bed," said the frog.

"I promise," said the princess.

So the frog jumped into the river and got the golden ball back.

The princess was so happy to have it back.

The next day, the frog jumped up to the castle.

"Princess, I would like to sit with you," he said.

"Yuck!" said the princess.

"If you make a promise, you must keep it," said the king.

So the princess let the frog sit with her.

Then the frog said,
"Princess, I would like
to eat with you, too."

"Yuck!" said the princess.

19

"You must keep your promise," said the king.

So the princess let the frog eat with her.

20

21

Then the frog said,
"I would like to sleep
on your bed, too."

"Yuck!" said the princess.

23

"You must keep your promise," said the king.

So the princess let the frog jump up on her bed.

24

Just then, the frog turned into a prince!

A spell had turned him into a frog. The princess had kept her promise and broken the spell.

The prince and
princess fell in love
and they got married.

They kept the golden
ball in the castle, too.

How much do you remember about the story of The Princess and the Frog? Answer these questions and find out!

- What does the princess drop in the river?

- Who tells the princess to keep her promise?

- Where does the frog want to sleep?

- What does the frog turn into?